Hairy Maclary's
SHOWBUSINESS

Lynley Dodd

TRICYCLE PRESS
Berkeley, California

In Riverside Hall
on Cabbage Tree Row,
the Cat Club were having
their Annual Show.

There were fat cats
and thin cats,
tabbies and grays,
kick-up-a-din cats
with boisterous ways.
Cooped up in cages,
they practiced their wails
while their owners fussed over
their teeth
and their
tails.

Out in the street,
tied to a tree,
Hairy Maclary
was trying to see.
He struggled and squirmed,
he unraveled the knot,
and dragging his lead,
he was off
at the
trot.

He bounced up the steps,
he pounced through the door,
he pricked up his ears,
and he pranced round the floor,
flapping and flustering,
bothering,
blustering,
leaving behind him
a hiss
and a
roar.

"STOP!"
cried the President,
"COLLAR HIM, QUICK!"
But Hairy Maclary
was slippery slick.

He slid under tables,

he jumped over chairs,

he skittered through legs,

and he sped down the stairs.

In and out doorways,
through banners and flags,

tangling together
belongings and bags.

Along came Miss Plum
with a big silver cup.
"GOT HIM!" she said
as she snaffled him up.

Preening and purring,
the prizewinners sat
with their rosettes and cups
on the prizewinners' mat...

and WHO
won the prize
for the SCRUFFIEST CAT?

Hairy Maclary
from Donaldson's Dairy.

Other TRICYCLE PRESS books by Lynley Dodd

Hairy Maclary from Donaldson's Dairy
Hairy Maclary's Bone
Hairy Maclary Scattercat
Hairy Maclary's Rumpus at the Vet
Hairy Maclary and Zachary Quack

Slinky Malinki
Slinky Malinki Catflaps
Slinky Malinki, Open the Door

TRICYCLE PRESS
an imprint of Ten Speed Press
PO Box 7123
Berkeley, California 94707
www.tricyclepress.com

Library of Congress Cataloging-in-Publication Data
Dodd, Lynley.
Hairy Maclary's showbusiness / by Lynley Dodd.
p. cm.
Summary: Fur rises and havoc ensues when Hairy Maclary the dog intrudes upon a cat show.
ISBN-13: 978-1-58246-208-0
ISBN-10: 1-58246-208-9
[1. Dogs—Fiction. 2. Cats—Fiction. 3. Stories in rhyme.] I. Title.
PZ9.3.D637Hajh 2006
[E—dc22
2006026642

First Tricycle Press printing, 2007
Printed in China

1 2 3 4 5 6 — 11 10 09 08 07